THE PATIO CLUB®

WRITTEN AND ILLUSTRATED BY

CARYN MOTTILLA

The *Lamp* *and the* *Leprechaun*

The Lamp and the Leprechaun
The Patio Club™
Published by Open Window Publishing
Castle Rock, CO

Publisher's Cataloging-in-Publication data

Names: Mottilla, Caryn, author.
Title: The Lamp and the Leprechaun / by Caryn Mottilla.
Description: First trade paperback original edition. Also available as an ebook. | Castle Rock [Colorado] : Open Window Publishing, 2019. | Series: The Patio Club.
Identifiers: ISBN 978-0-9997471-4-8
Subjects: LCSH: Old age—Fiction. | Leprechaun—Fiction. | Short stories.
BISAC: FICTION / General.
Classification: LCC PS374.O43 | DDC 813–dc22

Cover design by Caryn Mottilla

QUANTITY PURCHASES: Schools, companies, professional groups, clubs, and other organizations may qualify for special terms when ordering quantities of this title. For information, email ThePatioClub@gmail.com.

OPEN WINDOW
PUBLISHING

The Patio Club® is dedicated to the men and women in assisted living communities, memory and Hospice care who have listened to the adventures of The Patio Club®. They expressed their hope for these stories to be published and shared with others across the country.

Introducing the Patio Club

The Patio Club was originally formed by two sets of sisters—Elaine and Adele from New Jersey, and Betty and Mildred from Kentucky. The women were young when they met in the 1940s. The years passed by, and later in life, the four adventurous women made a pact that after they died they would meet up and visit retirement and assisted living communities. After they passed away, they came to Happy Visions Retirement Home and liked it so much they decided to stay.

The women call themselves "The Patio Club," because they sit outside on the patio of Happy Visions. Each day, Elaine, Adele,

Betty and Mildred are surrounded by colorful sparkles, and they meet a steady stream of interesting visitors and residents who pass through Happy Visions on their way to unknown destinations.

One amazing thing is that the Patio Club can look to the sky and watch a video of each person's life. This precious gift lets the Patio Club understand the unique story that each person carries with them.

The Lamp and the Leprechaun

IT WAS MID-MARCH AND SNOW WAS FALLING outside of Happy Visions Retirement Home. A tall oak tree in the front yard was quickly covered in sparkling white snow. Under the great tree's branches sat a young boy with red hair.

Suddenly, the boy walked over to the living room window and looked inside. He watched as the women of the Patio Club entered the living room and sat on the corduroy couches near the fireplace.

Elaine, Adele, Betty and Mildred were not aware that the young boy was watching them through the window as they talked about the snow storm. Elaine said, "Looks like March is coming in like a lion," and before she finished speaking, the young red-haired boy came in through the window and ran through the living room! The boy had red freckles on his face, and a trail of emerald green sparkles littered the floor behind him as he ran. Then the sparkles disappeared as quickly as the young boy.

The mischievous boy appeared to be about five years old and he was unfamiliar to the women of the Patio Club. Walter, the retirement home dog, was resting underneath the corduroy couch, and Walter's sensitive nose twitched as the young boy ran by him.

"Who was that?" asked Elaine. Before anyone could say anything, Elaine answered her own question. "Maybe it's one of the grandchildren who come here to visit."

As the excited women looked around the living room for the boy, they noticed a green lamp sitting on an end table next to the corduroy couch. The lamp was made of frosted green glass and had a lampshade covered in small, twinkling stars. A bronze leprechaun hung from a long chain and operated the lamp. The leprechaun seemed to invite everyone to pull the chain just to see what would happen.

Adele was seldom the first to try anything. However, she was the first one to reach for the bronze leprechaun. As she twirled it in her hand, Adele noticed the leprechaun's eyes.

"Look at this," Adele said excitedly. "The leprechaun has jewels for eyes, and they are the exact color of the green sparkles that trailed behind the young boy who just ran through here."

Elaine, Betty and Mildred quickly walked closer to inspect the lamp and the leprechaun. As they approached, Elaine said to the others, "I haven't seen this lamp before. Have you?"

"Well," said Betty, "today *IS* Saint Patrick's Day. Maybe it's a new decoration. I heard some of the residents talking about a leprechaun lamp, but I thought they were imagining things! A few of the residents guessed it had been brought to Happy Visions by one of the staff or one of the newest residents."

As the women of the Patio Club surrounded the green frosted glass lamp, it suddenly *buzzed* and flashed a bright lime-colored light throughout the living room. Needless to say, the women gasped with surprise, then started laughing. Even though the women of the Patio Club were surrounded each day by their own sparkles, the bright green flashing light still startled them!

Betty said, "Adele, unplug the lamp and let's take it outside to see if the video in the sky will give us some information." When Adele reached to unplug the lamp, she realized it was *not* plugged into an outlet.

"You will not believe this," whispered Adele to the others. "The leprechaun lamp is not plugged in. It is flashing all on its own!"

Mildred looked around to see if someone was playing a joke on them. After seeing no one, Mildred said, "Maybe the lamp belongs to Kathleen?"

Each day since Kathleen's arrival in early March, she walked the halls wearing long, white gloves and a dark green velvet gown. In her hand, she carried a small, green treasure chest the size of a recipe box, and it was trimmed in bronze. Kathleen smiled and waved to the residents each day like she was in a beauty pageant. The green leprechaun lamp looked like something Kathleen could have brought with her.

"Saint Patrick's Day," said Elaine. "Some things never change. People really enjoy the holiday that celebrates good luck and hidden fortunes. Maybe there is a fortune hidden somewhere."

Right after Elaine said this, the green lamp again flashed its vivid green light. "That must be true", said Betty. Thc four curious women carried the lamp out to the patio to watch the video in the sky, hoping it would tell the story of the green frosted glass lamp.

As the women left the living room, they saw Kathleen standing quietly in the corner of the room. She was wearing the green velvet gown and long, white gloves she wore each day. In her hand, she held the small, green treasure chest. Kathleen silently waved her other gloved hand to the ladies as she turned and left the room.

The women watched as Kathleen quickly walked through the hallway leading to the front door. A trail of green and gold sparkles dripped on the ground behind her like sparks from a welder's torch. As she walked, Kathleen's long, green velvet gown silently swept the trail of sparkles away.

At the end of the hallway, Kathleen went out the front door and joined hands with the red-haired boy the women had seen running through the living room. The boy was Kathleen's son, Georgie. He danced in the snow as green and gold sparks flew from the treasure chest his mother carried. Playfully, Georgie grabbed the small treasure chest and ran ahead of his mom.

Kathleen watched her young son as he ran through the snow to the large oak-tree in the front yard. The tree's branches seemed to wave softly to Georgie as he playfully buried the treasure chest in the snow at the base of the tree.

Kathleen went back inside and she could hear the cooks preparing the evening meal. Pots were clanging, and people were laughing as they worked. One of the cooks was Shannon. Everyone knew Shannon because she was always quick to give kind words and a hug to the residents.

Shannon had a generous spirit, but the money she earned cooking was just enough to pay her bills. However, if Shannon had one dollar for each hug and smile she gave to the residents, she would be able to retire early.

Outside, the four women of the Patio Club held the green lamp to the sky through the swirling snow. A video began to play and showed Kathleen in her green velvet

gown. She was lying on a bed, reading a story to her red-haired son. The boy giggled as his mom read to him by the light of a green glass lamp. As she read to him, the boy held tightly to a small, green treasure chest.

"That's Kathleen," said Betty. "Her son looks just like the boy who ran through the living room!"

"Look!" said Mildred. "It's the lamp. It has to be the same one we are holding right now." As she said this, the lamp suddenly flashed its bright green light, and it reflected off of the snow that was still falling.

As the video continued, the women heard Kathleen announce the story she was reading to her son. It was called, "*Georgie the Leprechaun.*" Her young son smiled and said what he always said when his mom read that story. "When I die, I am going to ask God if I can come back on Saint Patrick's Day as Georgie the Leprechaun. I will use a lamp to signal people and hide a treasure for someone special."

The video continued and showed Georgie in a hospital a few years later. His mother was reading the leprechaun story to him as he slept. Weeks later, young Georgie passed away.

There was a lively service to remember Georgie. People came to pay their respects, and saw a big picture of Georgie riding his green bicycle. Beside his picture was his favorite book, *Georgie the Leprechaun*. A small green treasure chest sat next to the book and was filled with chocolate coins wrapped in gold paper for each person to take home as a treat.

The video continued and showed the years that followed. Kathleen would ask Georgie each Saint Patrick's Day to give a treasure to someone in need. Knowing it would bring her son great joy, Kathleen began calling her son, "Georgie the Leprechaun,"—just like his favorite story.

Finally, the video showed Kathleen as she overheard Shannon telling someone on the phone that she didn't

have enough money to buy gas for the way home. Shannon joked and said, "Maybe a leprechaun will find me!" The video ended as Kathleen walked out the front door of Happy Visions.

By the time the women of the Patio Club finished watching the video, they were covered in snow—and so was the frosted green lamp.

Elaine was yelling to the other women, "Do you see? Georgie is here to give the treasure chest for Saint Patrick's Day to Shannon."

Quickly, the women went back inside and put the green lamp on the end table in the living room. They knew they did *not* need to plug it into an outlet.

Shannon was in the kitchen, and the women watched as Kathleen handed Shannon a card in a green envelope. Shannon smiled as she read the mystery card out loud to everyone in the kitchen:

"Go to the green frosted glass lamp in the living room, pull the leprechaun, and wait for your treasure." Shannon quickly hugged Kathleen as she ran to the living room.

Shannon passed the couch and went straight to the green frosted glass lamp. She did not know the lamp was unplugged as it flashed its bright lime green light throughout the room.

Elaine, Adele, Betty and Mildred watched with fascination as Shannon pulled the leprechaun chain on the lamp. "I hope she gets a lot more than gas money," said Adele.

Shannon waited with excitement and wondered if the little leprechaun really would bring her a fortune to pay for gas for her ride home. However, the light was her only surprise—*no treasure*!

As Shannon walked back to the kitchen, she heard the doorbell rang. One of the other cooks said they saw a small boy running through the front yard. "He is probably

playing a prank," Shannon said. "I will go and see what he is up to."

Kathleen stood quietly in the front hallway in her long, green velvet gown. She was smiling and sparkles of gold and emerald green fell to the floor around her. She watched as Shannon opened the front door.

Sitting on the welcome mat at the front door was a small, green leather treasure chest. As Shannon bent to pick it up, she thought she saw a brilliant green light around it. She looked in the distance and saw Georgie as he ran back to play in the snow at the base of the snow-covered tree.

Shannon opened the small, green treasure chest, and inside she saw a note with her name on it. The note read:

Dear Shannon,

Treasure will always find those who share the treasures of their hearts with others. This one is for you.

Love,

Georgie The Leprechaun

Underneath the plain green card were three shiny gold coins. Shannon picked them up, then ran back inside to tell the other staff members. "Look! A leprechaun left me a fortune! This is *real gold*, not chocolate candy!"

The Patio Club cheered as they heard of Shannon's good fortune. The average person may not believe in leprechauns. However, the luck of those who have a heart for others brings treasures every day.

Elaine, Adele, Betty and Mildred went one last time to watch the video as it played in the sky. This time, it showed Kathleen as she walked through the front door and across the drifting snow in the front yard. She met her son Georgie at the base of the old oak tree. Mother and son held hands and walked through the snow as Georgie carried the green treasure chest. Maybe next year they will return on Saint Patrick's Day to surprise someone special.

Happy Saint Patrick's Day from the Patio Club!

The End.

The Patio Club's Story

IN NOVEMBER OF 2016, I began writing fictional stories for retirement and assisted living communities. This occurred because of a simple request from an older gentleman in his 80s who asked if I could write a story about people "their age." Writing and telling stories has always come easily to me. I happily said , "yes." I was excited at the challenge and have written a story each month since then. They are about a fictional retirement/ assisted living community named *Happy Visions*. Each month I read to retirement and assisted living communities. The joy of doing this is overwhelming.

In July of 2017, I was reading to a group of older women as they sat outside *on the patio* in the shade. The women's ages reached up to 95. When I left the patio that day, I decided at that moment to write a story for them called "The Patio Club." The series began with that story.

The stories I write come effortlessly to me. It is as if I am divinely inspired. As I began writing the first story in the Patio Club series, I was so surprised as I watched the story come to life. It is the story of two sets of sisters, Elaine and Adele from New Jersey, and Mildred and Betty from Kentucky. They made a pact that when they died they would meet up and visit retirement and assisted living communities.

Imagine my surprise—because in real life Elaine and Adele (sisters) were my aunts from New Jersey, and Betty (my mother) and Mildred (my aunt) were sisters from Kentucky! My Aunt Mildred was the last one to join The Patio Club. She passed away earlier in 2017. The Patio Club™ stories now touch people from around the country and hopefully someday from around the world.

My dream is that The Patio Club™ series will be read to the people in assisted living, memory and Hospice care communities. As I read each month to these special people, I realized that it is often difficult to visit loved ones who are in the assisted living population. What I have found is that reading a story seems to transform everyone from the reader to the listener. I have seen people with all kinds of health challenges perk up when listening to the joyful adventures of The Patio Club™. They are in the present moment as they listen and during that time there is nothing wrong with them.

My wish is that people will take the adventure of reading a story (about 12 to 15 minutes) from The Patio Club Series to a loved one. It will transform the visit from one where it may be difficult to find something to talk about, to one where both the reader and listener are moved beyond words.

With gratitude and love,

- Caryn

Acknowledgments

THE PATIO CLUB is dedicated to my aunts Elaine, Adele, Mildred, and my mother Betty. Although the characters in the Patio Club are fictional, they are based on these important women who impacted my life.

Special thanks to my sons Carson and Cooper, as well as, family and friends who have listened to these stories. They have enthusiastically cheered for me to follow my dream to write and illustrate stories that bring joy and adventure to the lives of others.

Finally, I am grateful to God for the gifts He has given me to serve the people in assisted living, memory and Hospice care.

About the Author

CARYN BEGAN WRITING children's stories for her children in the 1990s. In 2016, as she read children's stories to assisted living communities, residents asked her to write a story "for people their age." That was how the adventure of writing for the adult and assisted population began.

Since that time, Caryn has written a monthly series called The Patio Club®. It takes place at a retirement home/assisted living community named Happy

Visions. The Patio Club™ are the first stories published by Caryn for that age group. The stories have captured the attention of people of all ages across the country.

The Patio Club™ stories are a bridge between the reader and the listener. Family and friends that visit assisted living, memory and Hospice care communities may struggle for something to talk about. Reading a story like The Patio Club™ to these special residents takes them on an adventure without them ever having to leave the room. It creates an opening for some interesting conversations!

Caryn lives in Colorado. She has two grown sons, Carson and Cooper

www.ingramcontent.com/pod-product-compliance
Lightning Source LLC
Chambersburg PA
CBHW041609120626
46551CB00002B/367